W9-BEV-571
12/18

EVERYDAY MINDFULNESS

Get Outdoors

Published in North America by Free Spirit Publishing Inc., Minneapolis, Minnesota, 2018

Library of Congress Cataloging-in-Publication Data
Names: Christelis, Paul, author. | Paganelli, Elisa, 1985- illustrator.
Title: Get outdoors : a mindfulness guide to noticing nature / written by Paul Christelis ; illustrated by Elisa Paganelli.
Description: Minneapolis, Minnesota : Free Spirit Publishing, 2018. | Series: Everyday mindfulness
Identifiers: LCCN 2017060598 | ISBN 9781631983337 (hardcover) | ISBN 1631983334 (hardcover)
Subjects: LCSH: Nature observation—Juvenile literature.
Classification: LCC QH48 .C567 2018 | DDC 508.072/3—c23 LC record available at https://lccn.loc.gov/2017060598

Reading Level Grade 2; Interest Level Ages 5–9; Fountas & Pinnell Guided Reading Level L

10 9 8 7 6 5 4 3 2 1
Printed in China
H13660518

Free Spirit Publishing Inc.
6325 Sandburg Road, Suite 100
Minneapolis, MN 55427-3674
(612) 338-2068
help4kids@freespirit.com
www.freespirit.com

First published in 2018 by Franklin Watts, a division of Hachette Children's Books • London, UK, and Sydney, Australia

Managing editor: Victoria Brooker
Creative design: Lisa Peacock

Get Outdoors

A MINDFULNESS GUIDE TO NOTICING NATURE

Written by
Paul Christelis

Illustrated by
Elisa Paganelli

free spirit
PUBLISHING®

WHAT IS MINDFULNESS?

Mindfulness is a way of paying attention to our present-moment experience with an attitude of kindness and curiosity. Most of the time, our attention is distracted—often by thoughts about the past or future—and this can make us feel jumpy, worried, self-critical, and confused.

By gently moving our focus from our busy minds into the present moment, we begin to let go of distraction and learn to tap into an ever-present supply of well-being and ease that resides in the here and now. Mindfulness can also help us improve concentration, calm unpleasant emotions, and even boost our immune systems.

In this book, children are encouraged to cultivate mindfulness by becoming curious about the natural world around them. By placing attention on their environment, they can quiet their distracted, worried, or self-critical minds.

Focusing on nature also reminds us that we are each connected to the wider world, which can help us feel more secure. This can also instill empathy for all living creatures and a sense of responsibility for the impact we make on the environment.

The book can be read interactively, allowing readers to pause at various points to turn their attention to what they are noticing. Watch for the PAUSE BUTTON in the text. It suggests opportunities to encourage readers to be curious about what they observe, whether this is outdoors, indoors, or an internal response to what they see, hear, smell, taste, or touch. Each time this PAUSE BUTTON is used, mindfulness is deepened.

Try not to rush this pause. Really allow enough time for children to stay with their experience. It doesn't matter if what they feel or notice is pleasant or unpleasant. What's important is to pay attention to it with a friendly attitude. This will introduce them to a way of being in the world that promotes health and happiness.

It's Saturday morning and Jada and her brother Michael are watching TV.

"That's all they ever seem to do!" sighs their dad. "It's a beautiful day and we are lucky enough to have a yard, but they won't budge from that couch!"

Suddenly, Dad has an idea. "Kids, who wants to win a prize?"
This gets their attention. "Me! Me!" they both shout.
"Then switch off the TV and listen up!" says Dad.

"You're going to play the Get Outdoors Game. The winner is the person who can notice the most **interesting** things outside. Each of you take a notebook and a pen to write down everything you see. And remember, sometimes the smallest things are the most interesting. So observe carefully!"

“What’s the prize?” asks Michael, who is very competitive.
“It’s a **surprise**,” says Dad.
“Now off you go. You have until lunchtime.”

PAUSE BUTTON

Do you have a yard or a park near your home? Take a moment to be curious about how much time you spend indoors and how much you spend outdoors.

“Hmm,” sighs Jada, looking at the yard.
“There’s not that much that’s interesting here.
All I see are the usual flowers and grass.”

“Try slowing down and
looking more closely,”
suggests Dad. “Sometimes,
things that are worth noticing
take time to see clearly.”

Let's take a peek at some of Michael's discoveries. Like Jada, he also sees flowers. But he **notices** so many different types!

Like Jada, Michael sees grass. But he also notices a blade that's been eaten by an ant and another blade with a dewdrop that's about to fall.

It's as if Michael's eyes have become magnifying glasses!

You can also turn your eyes into magnifying glasses! All you have to do is decide to look at things slowly and be really curious about what you're looking at. Try it now: Choose an object close by and spend some time looking at it carefully. Name all the small details that make this object unique.

Jada tries looking at the grass with curiosity
and this is what she sees:

Dad calls from the kitchen,
"Looking with your eyes is one way of taking notice of what's around you. But it's not the only way!"
Jada and Michael are puzzled. How else can they take notice?

PAUSE BUTTON

Can you think of other ways to pay attention to your environment? Here's a clue: It makes a lot of SENSE!

We notice by seeing, smelling, tasting, touching, and hearing: our five **senses**. Sometimes one sense is stronger, sometimes another. When we use our senses to pay attention, the whole world opens up for us in interesting ways.

Right now, Jada's using her sense of touch. She's kneeling on a wet clump of grass and her knees feel cold and a little itchy. "That's a good observation to write down!" she thinks.

Jada moves to a warmer, drier part of the yard. Her cold knees slowly begin to feel warm, like muffins being baked in an oven. She doesn't notice her knees very often. It feels good to notice them now!

Michael pauses to notice his sense of **touch**. The soft, moist grass cools his bare feet. There's an ant crawling over his elbow. It feels a little prickly!

PAUSE BUTTON

What do you notice right now with your sense of touch? Your clothes against your skin? Your fingers on the pages of this book? Being patient and curious will make this sense more powerful, so try not to rush your noticing.

"What happens when I switch to hearing?" wonders Jada. She moves her attention to her ears and listens.

At first, all she can hear is birdsong . . .

. . . but then she remembers to be patient and curious. She closes her eyes, which makes her sense of hearing even sharper.

Wow! Jada begins to notice so many other sounds.

And if she listens even more closely, she can tune into the **silence** in between sounds!

What sounds can you discover right now? All you need to do is close your eyes for about a minute, relax, and patiently wait for sounds to appear. You don't have to try to hear them: Let the sounds come to you. Say to yourself, "Welcome, sounds! I'm ready to hear you!" And if what you hear is silence, then let yourself listen to that.

While Jada is listening, Michael is on all fours in another part of the yard. Dad sees him from the kitchen window. “Is he pretending to be a dog?” he wonders.

With his nose in the flower bed,
Michael is using his sense of **smell**
to discover many different scents given off
by the flowers. Some smell sweet like honey,
others don't have a strong aroma . . .

. . . and then Michael smells a
strong, almost spicy odor that
makes his whole face crinkle
up. Ugh! The neighbor's dog
has been using the flower bed
as a toilet!

Nature is full of sights, **textures**, sounds, and smells. Some you might experience as pleasant, such as the feel of the warm sun on your skin. Some may be unpleasant, like the smell of dog poop. Some might not be pleasant or unpleasant, such as the sound of a passing car.

Just imagine what it would be like if we didn't have any of our senses to experience the world around us! We wouldn't notice very much, would we?

PAUSE BUTTON

Take a moment right now to really appreciate each of your senses.
What do you see?
What do you hear?
What do you notice with your sense of touch?
Can you smell anything?

"Wait a minute," says Michael. "We've forgotten something!" Jada realizes this too. "What is it?" She can almost remember. "It's on the tip of my tongue . . ."

Can you remember what Jada and Michael have forgotten? It's on the tip of your TONGUE too!

“Time for your surprise!” Dad calls. Jada and Michael run into the kitchen, leaving their notebooks on the grass.

“That’s it!” the children shout, feeling their mouths begin to water at the sight of a delicious, sweet cake. “Our sense of taste!”

NOTES FOR PARENTS AND TEACHERS

Here are a few mindfulness exercises and suggestions to add to children's Mindfulness Toolkits. These are simple, effective, and fun to do!

Senses in a Box

You can play this game with as many players as you'd like. Write down each of the four senses other than taste on four pieces of paper, fold them, and put them in a small box. When it's your turn, choose a piece of paper from the box. Read out the sense that's written on that paper. If, for example, you have picked *smell*, then set a timer for three minutes. During this time, all players should use their sense of smell to pay attention to what's around them. Write down all of your observations, just as Jada and Michael did in the story. At the end of the three minutes, spend some time sharing what you noticed. What was the most common smell? The most pleasant? Unpleasant? Unusual? Then choose a different player to pick a new sense from the box.

If you really want to sharpen your attention during this game, try playing it in silence. Talking can dilute our attention and distract us from noticing things.

This game is best played outdoors to take advantage of the endless wonders of nature around us. However, if it's not possible to be outside, exploring indoors can work well too. What's important is to remain curious and open to our environment, wherever we may be.

Be a Tree

This practice is a meditation that encourages children to embrace stillness and be receptive to what's around them.

Choose a spot outside, preferably where trees are present. Encourage children to stand or sit up straight and to be still and relaxed, just like a tree. They can imagine that they have roots growing from under their feet into the earth. They can spread their fingers and notice the feel of the breeze or wind moving past their hands, just like wind passing through tree branches. This is especially effective with closed eyes, allowing children to deeply experience the feeling of being still and quiet in the open, and allowing them to hear the sounds around them.

Super Sense Spot

A variation of the tree meditation is to sit down on the ground and to claim that spot as your Super Sense Spot. Notice how it feels to make contact with the earth. Then look around you and take in as many sights, smells, and sounds as you can. Remember to look above at the sky and notice shapes and textures of clouds, the shade of blue or gray, birds passing overhead, and so on.

Notice that if you sit for long enough you observe different things. In fact, it is important to really give yourself enough time for this exercise, because initially the first few minutes can seem unremarkable. It's only when we slow down our attention that we start to pay attention to all the little sensations that are going on in and around us.

What's great about these mindfulness practices is that there is no such thing as a right or wrong "answer." Simply allow children to have their own responses to stimuli. Help them be curious about how they experience the world by entering into the experience with them through prompts like: "Tell me more about that." "How does that sunset make you feel inside?" "What's it like to be as still as a tree?" Share your own responses too. This helps children accept and validate others' experiences, even if they differ from theirs.

BOOKS TO SHARE

Acorns to Great Oaks: Meditations for Children by Marie Delanote, illustrated by Jokanies (Findhorn Press, 2017)

Breathe and Be: A Book of Mindfulness Poems by Kate Coombs, illustrated by Anna Emilia Laitinen (Sounds True, 2017)

Breathe Like a Bear: 30 Mindful Moments for Kids to Feel Calm and Focused Anytime, Anywhere by Kira Willey, illustrated by Anni Betts (Rodale Kids, 2017)

I Am Peace: A Book of Mindfulness by Susan Verde, illustrated by Peter H. Reynolds (Abrams Books for Young Readers, 2017)

Sitting Still Like a Frog: Mindfulness Exercises for Kids (and Their Parents) by Eline Snel (Shambhala Publications, 2013)

Visiting Feelings by Lauren Rubenstein, illustrated by Shelly Hehenberger (Magination Press, 2014)

What Does It Mean to Be Present? by Rana DiOrio, illustrated by Eliza Wheeler (Little Pickle Stories, 2010)

A World of Pausabilities: An Exercise in Mindfulness by Frank J. Sileo, illustrated by Jennifer Zivoin (Magination Press, 2017)